It's Christmas and Daisy has been given an
actual part in the actual school Christmas play!
She has special lines to learn and even a
special costume to wear!!

TROUBLE is . . . there's something about baby
Jesus that isn't quite special enough.

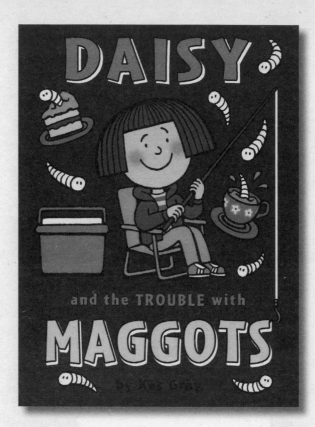

Look out ducks, look out canoeists . . . Daisy is
going fishing for the very first time ever! She's got
an actual fishing rod that catches actual fish,
an actual bait box full of actual maggots.

TROUBLE is, she's got an actual fishing catapult
that pings, twangs, BLAMS . . . oh dear.

Praise for Jack Beechwhistle:

"I wish he'd joined us instead."
Head of MI5

"You can run, you can hide, but if
you're a baddie he will find you."
Chief of the Canadian Mounties

"His name is Beechwhistle.
Jack Beechwhistle."
J. Bond

"Get me Jack Beechwhistle."
Head of the FBI

"Is there no mission too big
for this boy, gurgle?"
King of Venus

www.randomhouse.co.uk

JACK BEECHWHISTLE

ATTACK of the GIANT SLUGS

by Kes Gray

RED FOX

RED FOX

UK I USA I Canada I Ireland I Australia
India I New Zealand I South Africa

Red Fox is part of the Penguin Random House group of companies whose addresses can
be found at global.penguinrandomhouse.com.

www.penguin.co.uk
www.puffinbooks.co.uk
www.ladybird.co.uk

Penguin
Random House
UK

First published 2016

003

Text copyright © Kes Gray, 2016
Cover illustration © Nick Sharratt, 2016
Inside illustrations © Garry Parsons, 2016

The moral right of the author and illustrators has been asserted.

Set in Vag Rounded 15/23pt
Printed and bound in Great Britain by Clays Ltd, St Ives plc

A CIP catalogue record for this book is available from the British Library.

ISBN: 978-1-782-95303-6

Penguin Random House is committed to a sustainable future for our business, our readers
and our planet. This book is made from Forest Stewardship Council® certified paper.

MIX
Paper from
responsible sources
FSC® C018179

To wet bums and muddy shoes.

CHAPTER 1

Hi. Don't panic, but you're in danger. Or at least you would be if I wasn't around to look out for you. The name's Jack Dragon Beechwhistle, Junior Defender of the World. Adult High Command call me Agent J. You can call me Jack.

I've been doing undercover world defence work for about three years. I was recruited by my dad. He does secret work for the government too.

You don't have to believe me if you don't want to. The important thing is that you're safe.

I guess you could say there is danger in my blood. In the last three years I've saved the world about twenty-seven times – from alien attacks, zombie sweet-shop owners, poisonous footballs, man-eating post boxes, exploding conkers – but I don't want any thanks for it. Thanks aren't my style. And anyway, if a load of medals were pinned to my jumper, the weight of them would only slow me down. Or give me away. Especially like if I was holed out in the desert and my medals flashed in the sun.

When the work you do is top secret as well as top dangerous, it's important that you blend in with the crowd. That's why I wear a school uniform five days of the week and jeans at the weekend. If I didn't have to work undercover, I'd probably wear a one-piece armoured suit like Iron Man. Only I'd have a drinks holder on the shoulders of both arms.

The drink I'd put in my drinks holders is Lucozade Sport because it aids recovery. Recovering from some of my missions would take weeks if I only had normal squash to drink when I got home. With Lucozade Sport, enemies can throw anything at me and I'm just ready to go again.

If I told you where I lived, I would be putting your life at risk. There are a lot of bad people looking for me and there is no telling what they'd do to you if they found out you had the information they needed.

I can tell you I live in a house. But it's a house different to any other house on my street. My front door looks red, but that's a disguise; its real colour is hidden in a layer of paint underneath. The number on my door says 38, but that isn't the real number either.

Open my front gate, and a high-pitched sonic intruder warning alarm will tell me that someone is approaching. Ring my doorbell, and the fingerprint of the finger that is pushing the button will automatically be sent to my computer files.

All the windows are bulletproof. The double-glazing people who fitted them were world defence agents in disguise. But the best thing about my house is the chimney. If it all kicks off, you'd better watch out for my chimney. Especially if you're a giant slug.

CHAPTER 2

Do you ever go out? If you don't, you should do because outside is where it's at. If you think about it, all you're ever gonna find inside a house is boring stuff like sofas and armchairs and carpets and beds and sinks full of washing-up. It's always the same old stuff. Outside, nothing is ever the same. There's rain and snow and sun and wind and mud and dirt and stingers and trees and ditches and dens and puddles and ponds and rubbish dumps and burned-out cars and gangster hideouts and zombie caves and everything.

When you're outside, anything can happen: volcanoes can erupt, earthquakes can rumble, tsunamis can hit, meteors can collide, forest fires can burn. You have to be on the lookout for danger signals every single second of the day, especially if you go to the kind of places I go.

I'm talking the Blackberry Maze.
I'm talking the Devil's Weir,
the Dark Dark Woods,
Hangman's Stream,

the Bomb Hole,

Scorched Urf,

Hell Hill,

Allotment 24

and Dino Valley.

There's nowhere a world defence mission can't take me. And as long as it isn't later than eight o'clock at night, there's nowhere that Harry and Colin won't follow.

Harry Bayliss and Colin Kettle are my best friends. We live on the same street. We're in the same class at school too. We hang out together, play football, go exploring, climb trees, build dens – and when we're called into action, we go on missions.

Harry and Colin would follow me anywhere, 'cos we've made a blood pact. We didn't use real blood. We used squashed-up berry juice. (Hawthorn berries are the best.) Sounds a bit strange, I know, but if there really is danger in my blood, then it wouldn't be fair to share it with Harry and Colin.

The missions we go on are totally full-on. To survive them, you need combat skills, tracking skills, survival skills, escaping skills, dirty-water-drinking skills, alien skills, tramp skills, and other skills that are so skilful they take hundreds of missions to learn.

I've told Harry and Colin that when I've finished training them up, they could get to become proper agents like me. Except at the moment they can't, because they have to be in bed by eight o'clock every night. Even on weekends.

Qualified junior world defence agents don't have bedtimes. They have to be available every second of every minute of every hour 24/7/12/365, because that's when the enemy can strike.

But try telling Harry and Colin's parents that.

Harry and Colin are a bit unlucky really: they both have the wrong kind of parents – you know, the kind of parents who worry about their children all the time.

My mum and dad don't worry about me all the time. In fact my mum and dad don't worry about me at all. Because they know I can look after myself.

Harry did try sneaking out of his bedroom window to go on a mission with me one night, but he lost his grip on the drainpipe and fell through his conservatory roof.

Luckily he had his gloves on, and his bomber jacket and balaclava, so he was pretty well padded when he hit the ground. His mum and dad went mental when they saw all the broken glass, though.

They didn't see me. I was hanging Batman-style from the swing in Harry's garden when it happened. But you'd never have known I was there, because I was dressed in my shadow gear too.

Shadow gear is one of the most important things to have if you're doing night-time world defence missions, because the darkness of your clothes helps you blend into the darkness of the night.

You wouldn't believe some of the places I've been in my shadow gear without anybody seeing me.

My shadow gear is basically a black hoodie, a black T-shirt,

 a black scarf,

black jeans,

black gloves,

and black trainers
with yellow glow-
in-the-dark laces.

Sometimes I wear
black socks too.

In case you're wondering why my laces are yellow glow-in-the-dark and not black, it's because if I ever have to climb up a snake-filled tree in the dead of night, or a guarded castle wall or a steep, rocky cliff-face, and Harry and Colin are following in my footsteps, my glow-in-the-dark laces will lead the way. Or at least they would do if Harry and Colin were allowed to come with me.

Harry and Colin have asked me if I can get letters sent to their parents from High Command, ordering them to let their children go to bed whenever they like. But

I've told them it's too risky. If High Command sent the letters to Harry and Colin's parents and they were intercepted by enemy agents, then Harry and Colin's families would all be put at risk, including Colin's baby sister and Harry's gerbils.

They might even try and use the letters from High Command to get to ME.

I reckon in total I've nearly been properly kidnapped about twelve times, by all kinds of different enemies. I've always managed to escape though, because I'm brilliant at getting out of enemy holds.

Combat holds and how to get out of them are one of my specialities. In fact I was teaching holds to Harry and Colin last Saturday morning, when the attack of the giant slugs began.

That's the thing about monster invasions. They can start anywhere, at any time. Even in the middle of a double headlock down by the rhubarb on Allotment 24.

CHAPTER 3

I don't know what you do on Saturday mornings, but me, Harry and Colin always get up early. Getting up early means you've got the whole day to go exploring, save the world or do your training.

Last Saturday morning started pretty normally for me. I got up, got dressed and sniffed the milk. I like milk, but I don't like milk with lumps.

Lumpy milk isn't just hard to swallow –
it makes my nose jump when I sniff it.

The milk in my house gets lumpy
all the time. Not because it's old,
but because my mum and dad keep
forgetting to put it back in the fridge
when they get back from the pub.

I never wake my mum and dad up at the weekend because they get really grumpy if I do. They like to have a lie-in on Saturdays. And Sundays. Sometimes they don't get up until the afternoon.

Saturday and Sunday mornings are definitely the worst times in my house for lumpy milk, but last Saturday the milk smelled and tasted OK. Which was good, because milk is one of the best things you can drink before going on a training mission.

When I went out to the garage to get my bike, I noticed that it had been raining during the night. My

saddle was wet because I'd left my bike propped up against the wall, but once I'd wiped it with my hoodie sleeve, I was good to go.

When I got to the end of my driveway, I found Colin and Harry already sitting on their bikes waiting for me. They were both dressed the same: black jeans, green hoodies, black trainers. Harry and Colin always dress the same at weekends. It's kind of like their uniform.

There are loads of different places we can go to do our world defence training. That morning I'd decided to teach Harry and Colin jungle headlocks, so it had to be Allotment 24.

Allotment 24 is one of the neatest places on Earth. It's overgrown, just like a jungle, it has a secret tap that we can use to fill our drinks bottles, and it's got a shed that looks like you can't get in, but we can, because we've made a secret way in.

It's about a fifteen-minute bike ride to Allotment 24 – ten minutes if we take a short cut through the Blackberry Maze and cut across Scorched Urf. Last Saturday morning we had to go the long way because Colin's mum and dad had run out of bread. On Saturday mornings Colin always brings the bread. Harry brings the sauce and I bring the bacon.

In case you don't know what an allotment is, it's a place where people who haven't got gardens grow their vegetables; kind of like a big field covered in brown squares of earth.

The squares on the allotment are numbered 1 to 46. No one has been growing vegetables on Allotment 24 for years.

Apparently Allotment 24 will never have vegetables planted on it again. Not because the soil is poisonous or full of killer worms, but because the whole square is covered with a really bad weed called notweed.

Why it's called notweed if it is a weed, I don't know. But I do know that if you get it in your garden, you'd better drop your watering can and run. Because not only is notweed really fast-growing; its stalks are so powerful, they can bend a gardener's spade with their bare leaves.

Some people believe that notweed doesn't even come from this planet. Colin reckons that the red bits on its stalks mean that the seeds might have sprinkled down from Mars, possibly in a meteor shower. Harry reckons they might have come into the Earth's atmosphere on the soles of an astronaut's boot.

Anyway, whoever planted notweed on Allotment 24 never lived to tell the tale because they got grabbed by the leaves before they could even empty their wheelbarrow.

The lost gardener of Allotment 24 has never been seen since.

Only his shed remains.

CHAPTER 4

The first time we discovered the empty shed on Allotment 24 we thought we would be able to make it our den straight away. But the best dens are never that simple.

To make a den a secret den, it's no use bashing off the padlock or kicking in the door because that means anyone who comes along can get into it too. What you need with a secret den is a way in that only you can use.

It took us over a week to dig the tunnel.

The tunnel we've dug to get into our den starts at the back of the shed, goes down about half a metre, then through, up and inside. Or at least, it does now that we've made a hole in the wood of the shed floor. That was the hardest bit – breaking through the planks to get inside.

SECURITY TIP: Make sure that the entrance to your den is only big enough for you to squeeze through, otherwise enemies could crawl in and get you.

Allotment 24
our shed
shelves
way in
lift off lid
window
Door
old fork
water butt
flower pots
bottles
Jars

Colin and Harry did most of the early digging, but I was the first one to actually break through. When I got my head inside and looked up into the shed, it was one of the best moments I've ever had. The space inside couldn't have been more perfect. It had empty shelves, it had hooks, it had glass jars and empty bottles with screw-on lids, and it was easily big enough for all three of us to sit down and stretch out our legs.

SURVIVAL TIP: If your den is a shed on an allotment, cover your tunnel entrance with a hollowed-out water butt. This will make your entrance twice as secret and give you something with a lid to climb through as well.

It even had a rusty garden fork, which was a good job, because that was what I had to use to kill the giant spider that attacked me as I heaved myself up through the hole.

I'm guessing you've never been attacked by a giant spider. If you have, then you'll know what a fight you have to put up to defeat one, especially giant spiders with glowing red eyes.

They were the first thing I saw: two red eyes, dropping like red yoyos from the cobwebs that were hanging from the ceiling. At first I thought I was going to have to wrestle the hairy beast with my bare hands, but when I saw the rusty garden fork propped up below one of the windows, I knew what I had to do.

The rest is history.

By the time Harry and Colin had crawled through the tunnel and up into the shed to join me, the danger was sorted. Plus the giant spider had shrunk back down to its normal size. That's what giant spiders do if you stab them in their weak spot, just below their fangs. They die, then they shrink back to the size of a normal spider, only slightly smaller because only their skeleton is left.

Harry said we should leave the shrunken spider skeleton in the web across the window to remind us that danger is always lurking. Colin said we should keep it in a jar as a trophy. But I said they both had a lot to learn. Because even though you can kill a giant spider, you can never stop its dead radio waves bleeping out from inside its bones.

When I told Harry and Colin that even though the spider was dead it could still send out distress signals through its web to other giant spiders nearby, we all agreed what we had to do. We had to start clearing all the cobwebs out of the shed and we had to do it fast.

Luckily none of us are afraid of hard work, or allergic to cobwebs, dead butterflies and curled-up wasps. After a couple of hours the job was done. The shed was clean, the flowerpots were cleared out and our best-ever discovery was discovered.

Think bread. Think sauce. Think bacon . . .

Think the lost gardener of Allotment 24's very own camping stove!

CHAPTER 5

We've been using the lost gardener of Allotment 24's camping stove to cook our breakfast every Saturday morning since our den finally became ready.

It was Harry who found the camping stove and it was Colin who found the matches. But it was me who showed them how to cook bacon.

I've been cooking bacon by myself since I was about seven. It was my mum who taught me how to do it, just in case she wasn't there when I got home from school.

When we got to Allotment 24 last Saturday, my hunger juices were already gurgling. I think it was because I'd only had one piece of bacon for my tea the night before – my mum had been called out on another mission with my dad. There were other bits of bacon in the fridge I could have eaten, but I had to make sure I still had six left for the morning.

That's the way we always do our sandwiches on Saturday mornings – two rashers of bacon each.

CAMO TIP: When you get to your den, cover your bikes with broken branches to camouflage them while you are not using them. This will stop the enemy from finding and stealing them or spy planes spotting them from the air.

The best thing about cooking bacon sandwiches in a secret den is the smell. Especially if you let the bacon sizzle till it goes crispy.

While we were eating our bacon sandwiches, I told Harry and Colin about the training sessions I had planned for the day.

First of all we would be doing double headlocks by the rhubarb.

Then I would show them how to fight off ambushers in a jungle.

Then we would practise parachute jumps off the roof of our den.

Then, depending on how much time we had left, we might go over to Hangman's Stream to jump some rapids, or maybe Dino Valley to trap some raptors.

It had started raining again, but we were really keen to get started. In fact we were so keen, we almost forgot to put the lid back on the water butt once we'd climbed out!

Usually when we start our training sessions, we flip a coin to see if Harry or Colin will train with me first. But with double-headlock lessons, you need two people to do headlocks on at the same time, so there was no need to flip a coin at all.

You might have seen double headlocks before. They sometimes do them in the wrestling on the telly. But don't be fooled, because the double headlocks that I teach are totally for real.

My best three double headlocks
of all time are:

aliens

saltwater crocodiles

headless ghosts

To make our training like real life,
I told Harry and Colin to change their
names, stand by the rhubarb and
pretend to be Dark Force sentries.

Once they'd got their sentry names worked out, I told them they needed to think of something to talk about while I was secretly creeping up on them. Otherwise, when I got them in a double headlock, it wouldn't be a total surprise.

Colin had just the idea:

That's right, Zyborg. The Kingdom of Rhubarbia must prepare for attack.

RHUBARBIA'S BULLET MAKERS HAD BEEN WORKING THROUGH THE NIGHT, BUT WHAT GOOD WOULD BULLETS BE AGAINST . . .

. . . DOUBLE HEADLOCKS?

I had them! I had climbed the Mountain of Grimdor, swum the River of Blud, hacked my way through the Forest of Dredd, crept up on the entrance to Rhubarbia from the west, and headlocked both sentries in one pounce!

"How did you sneak up behind us?!" gurgled Thranx as I wrestled him and Zyborg to the ground. "Our backs were right up against the door!"

"SKILL AND SPEED!" I laughed. "SKILL AND SPEED!!!!"

My surprise rebel tactics had totally worked. All I had to do now was get both sentries to submit.

Zyborg was the first to surrender.

"I give up," he gasped, "your headlock skills are too awesome!"

Zyborg was right – once I had them in my special grip, there was no way I could be beaten.

"Give me the keys to the Kingdom doors!" I commanded.

"NEVER!" gasped Thranx. "I'll never let you past!"

"GIVE ME THE KEYS, OR ELSE!" I ordered, tightening my locks on both heads.

"You'll never take me alive!" gasped Thranx, putting up much more resistance than I'd expected.

"That can be arranged!" I smiled.

"UUURRRGGGGGHHH," gurgled Thranx, as I dragged his brave face closer to the Rhubarbian ground.

"SEE WHAT YOU'RE UP AGAINST!" I laughed.

"OOOER!?" gurgled Harry, suddenly going all floppy and pointing at the wet grass.

"OOOER, WHAT?" I said, relaxing my grips on Colin and Harry's heads and crawling into the rhubarb for a closer look.

"There!" pointed Colin.

"Gross," shivered Harry.

"SLUGS!" I shuddered. "SLUGS UPON SLUGS UPON SLUGS! FOR REAL!"

CHAPTER 6

If there's one thing I've learned during all the training sessions and secret missions I've been on, it's to expect the unexpected. Wherever you are, whatever you are doing, you have to be one hundred per cent ready for the unexpected to suddenly and unexpectedly happen.

We'd all seen slugs before, but never this many all at once.

"Maybe the rain has brought them out," said Colin.

"Maybe," I said, letting go of both

headlocks and crawling forward on my elbows for a closer look.

I counted seventeen slugs underneath the rhubarb, bodies sliming, feelers waving and mouths munching.

"Why are there so many?" asked Colin.

"What are they eating?" asked Harry.

It wasn't rhubarb.

"It's a blackbird!" I said, leaning forward so close that raindrops from on the rhubarb leaves went dribbling down my neck. "It's a dead blackbird. Look! There's a leg, those are feathers and there's what's left of its wing."

The closer I looked, the better

I saw. The pile of soggy black stuff under the rhubarb was definitely the remains of a dead blackbird. I could tell by the yellow beak.

"It must have been there for weeks," said Harry, shoving his cheek right up close to mine.

"I didn't know slugs ate meat," said Colin, scrambling forward for an even closer look. "I thought slugs only ate green stuff."

"Or mouldy yellow and brown stuff," said Harry.

"If something is rotting, I guess a slug will eat it," I said, jumping back onto the track beside the allotment and then standing up to stretch my legs.

"Do you think they'd make good pets?" said Colin, pulling a leaf from a notweed stalk and then using it to nudge a slug towards him.

"They're too sticky to be a pet," I said. "And slimy."

"Do you reckon they could hear you if you called them?"

"I'm not sure they've got any ears," said Harry. "Have slugs got ears, Jack?" he asked.

Even after all the global missions I'd been on, it wasn't a question that I was able to answer.

"If they had ears, you could teach them commands," said Colin. "If they had paws, you could get them to beg."

"If they weren't so sticky, you could teach them to roll over!" laughed Harry.

"Yeah, if a slug tried to roll over it would get stuck half way!" said Colin.

My men were losing their discipline.

"ATTENTION!" I shouted. "HAVE YOU FORGOTTEN WHY WE'RE HERE? ON YOUR FEET THIS INSTANT! EYES RIGHT AND PREPARE FOR JUNGLE TRAINING!"

CHAPTER 7

If one thing is guaranteed to take your mind off slugs, it's the thought of jungle training. Especially *my* jungle training.

Ambushers are some of the sneakiest enemies you can fight, because not only do they dress the same colour as the jungle, they jump out on you the moment you go to the back of the line. Especially in a jungle that's thick with leaves.

I've been grabbed by ambushers in African jungles, Indian jungles, Chinese jungles and Russian jungles. I even got grabbed by a yeti ambusher once when I was at the end of a long rope of world defence agents climbing Mount Everest. Luckily I've always got away, because my ambush skills are so good.

There are three types of ambush skills that a world defence agent has to learn:

Reaction skills: the quicker you react to being grabbed by an ambusher, the better chance you have of getting away.

Shouting skills: the louder you shout when an ambusher grabs you, the quicker the people in front of you will know that the ambush is happening.

Pressure-point skills: the sooner you get the ambusher by their pressure points, the sooner the ambusher will let go of you.

PRESSURE-POINT TIP:

Pressure points are special places on ambushers' bodies that make them fall asleep the instant you press them. But remember, pressure points aren't always in the same place. It depends on the type of ambusher ambushing you.

Before we entered the Jungle of Lost Souls, I briefed Harry and Colin on the dangers that lay ahead. Jungle soldiers would try and ambush them round the neck, hissing snakes would try and grab them by the ankle, combat chameleons would try and drop down on them from the trees above, and cannibal gorillas would come at them from all directions and then try and carry them off and turn them into bacon.

Then I told them where the pressure points on each of the different baddies could be found.

Jungle soldiers: halfway between the shoulder and elbow of the left arm.

Hissing snakes: right in the middle of its hissing tongue.

Combat chameleon: the curliest bit of its tail.

Cannibal gorilla: right in the middle of its furry forehead.

"So you're going to be leading us from the front?" asked Harry.

"That's right," I said, "because I'm not the one who's being ambushed."

"And me and Harry are going to take it in turns to walk at the back?"

"That's right," I said, "because you ARE the ones who'll be being ambushed."

"How will we know when we've been ambushed?" asked Harry.

"I'll shout 'AMBUSH!'" I said.

"And how will we know what kind of enemy is ambushing us?" asked Colin.

"I'll shout 'JUNGLE SOLDIER!' or 'HISSING SNAKE!' or 'COMBAT

CHAMELEON!' or 'CANNIBAL GORILLA!'"
I said. "And when I do, you have to
turn round really fast and grab the
enemies by the right pressure points.
If you squeeze the wrong pressure
points, you'll be dead!"

It was a lot for Harry and Colin to
get their heads around, but listening
carefully to my instructions would
mean the difference between them
coming out the other side of the jungle
alive or not.

At 10.15 hundred hours precisely
we formed a line, synchronized our
watches, parted the jungle leaves
and got ready to step in.

BRAVELY, THEY ENTERED THE JUNGLE OF LOST SOULS.

CHAPTER 8

Things went well for the first hour or so. Colin and Harry were quick at turning round when they were ambushed, and they were excellent at remembering which pressure points to squeeze.

It was a good job I had trained them well too, because the deeper we got into the jungle, the more dangerous things became. Ambushers were everywhere. We had to watch our backs, our fronts, our sides, our aboves and our belows.

But even that didn't prepare us for the HISSING GORILLA.

The moment I shouted, "HISSING GORILLA!" I knew that Colin would be confused, because hissing gorillas are a cross between cannibal gorillas and hissing snakes. Which makes them the rarest gorillas on the planet. Plus it means their pressure points aren't on their furry forehead or the middle of their hissing tongue, they are halfway in between.

Which meant that Colin wouldn't know which pressure point to press!

COLIN WAS CAPTURED!

HARRY WAS CAPTURED!

Squeeze its nose!

By the time I had shouted, "SQUEEZE ITS NOSE!" Colin was already in a death hold. Not only that – Harry had been grabbed by a COMBAT SNAKE!

"SQUEEZE ITS POO HOLE!" I shouted to Harry. "HALFWAY BETWEEN ITS HISSING TONGUE AND THE TIP OF ITS CURLY TAIL!"

But it was too late.

Harry had been bitten on the leg and the poison from the fangs of the angry combat snake had gone into his blood, up his veins and was heading for his brain!

Thank goodness I've been trained to think and act fast in emergency situations.

Quick as a flash, I squeezed the hissing gorilla's nose, just seconds before he had a chance to squeeze the last breath of oxygen from Colin's lungs. In an instant the hissing gorilla was asleep on the floor and Colin was saved.

All I had to do now was save Harry.

The combat snake was a huge angry reptile with armour-plated skin and yellow fangs. It had wrapped its coils around Harry's body so tightly, it meant I couldn't even see where its pressure points might be!

"TAKE THAT!" I shouted, tying the tip of the combat snake's curly tail in a knot and then wedging it between two tree branches. "SPIN, HARRY!" I shouted. "Spin round and round AS FAST AS YOU CAN before the poison can take hold!"

As soon as Harry started to spin, the snake began to unwind.

"TAKE THAT!" I shouted, squeezing

the combat snake's pressure points as soon as I could see them.

"AND THAT!" I shouted, pulling the fangs out of its sleeping mouth and keeping them as a trophy.

It had been one of my closest jungle calls ever, but I had pulled it off. I had saved Colin from the grip of a hissing gorilla and I had freed Harry from the fangs of a humungous combat snake.

"I owe you, Jack!" gasped Colin, filling his lungs with fresh air.

"Man down," gasped Harry, dropping unconscious to the jungle floor.

CHAPTER 9

POISON FACT FILE:

Poison: One of the most poisonous things on Earth.

Combat snake poison: THE most poisonous poison in the entire universe.

"Hang on in there, buddy," I said, propping Harry up against a tree to make him more comfortable. "I'm going to make some medicine that will save you."

This is the way a training session can go sometimes. One minute you are teaching ambush skills, the next minute the poison from a combat snake's fangs kicks in and you find yourself in a life-or-death situation, having to teach medicine skills instead.

There are about 150 different medicines I could tell you about. The medicine I needed to save Harry from a combat snakebite would be the hardest I'd ever had to make. I was going to need special leaves, hard-to-find twigs, purple beetle wings, really rare tree bark, caterpillar hairs, monkey's breath and magic spring water from the centre of the Earth.

Luckily, everything we needed could be found in the jungle we had just been ambushed in. All I had to do was send Colin out to find all the ingredients and mix them together when he got back FAST!

"Colin," I said, "I'm putting Harry's life in your hands. Here is a list of magic things to find. Find them fast and there is every chance I will be able to mix a potion that will bring Harry back from the brink. Find them slow and we could lose him. Now, GO FIND!"

When Colin started coming back with the wrong caterpillars, I knew I was going to have to find everything myself. It wasn't his fault. In situations like this, only properly qualified junior world defence agents like me would have enough jungle experience to know exactly where to look.

"Check out that wollibob tree," I shouted. "Look inside bat droppings for purple beetles' wings!"

Harry was in a bad way. The poison was up to his eyeballs now, and if I didn't act fast, we would lose him for sure. Luckily, I made the antidote just in time.

The moment Harry drank it, he sat up and his eyes began to flicker.

"Where am I?" he said.

"The Jungle of Lost Souls, " I told him.

"What happened?" he asked.

"Bad snakebite," Colin explained.

We had nearly lost Harry, but when we got back to our den, thanks to my jungle knowledge and Colin's fast collecting skills, we were still a three-man team.

"I'll tell you what else I saw in the jungle when I was collecting things for the antidote," Colin said.

"What did you see?" I asked as we laid Harry down on the grass. I was expecting him to say parrots, or lemurs or flying foxes.

"More slugs," said Colin.

CHAPTER 10

I didn't have a chance to ask Colin about the slugs he'd seen in the jungle, because it was time for our parachute training session.

Harry could stand up on his own now, without any help from us at all. His eyes had stopped flickering, his legs had stopped shaking, and he was totally ready for a flight to the North Pole.

In fact, both Harry and Colin were

so ready, they had already taken their seats on the plane!

READY FOR TAKE-OFF!

I'd chosen the North Pole to fly to because our next training session wasn't just normal parachute jumping, it was parachuting with one important difference.

No parachutes.

If you've ever parachuted into enemy territory, then you will know how dangerous parachuting can be. Not just because the enemy could be firing missiles at you when you jump, but because if your parachute doesn't open when you pull your cord, you won't be parachuting at all. You'll be falling through the sky at about a hundred miles an hour.

The first time I ever realized how dangerous this could be was when I was doing a parachute mission over Washington, DC. It was about two years ago. The President of the United States had been taken prisoner in the White House and I had been asked to go in and set him free.

I had been flown out from a secret airbase in England, told exactly which room in the White House the President had been tied up in and which secret tunnels I needed to crawl through to save him.

The skies were clear, visibility was good, my jump out of the plane was perfect, and everything was going totally to plan.

Until I pulled my parachute cord.

The instant I pulled the cord and my parachute didn't open, I knew that I was in trouble. The instant I pulled my emergency cord and even my back-up parachute didn't open, I knew that I was in BIG, BIG trouble.

Luckily I remembered to bend my knees when I hit the White House lawn.

Bending your knees when you land on the ground is the only way you will ever survive a parachute jump with no parachute. You'll have an even better chance of surviving if you bend your knees and roll over.

I must have rolled over and over about twenty times when I landed on the White House lawn, which was really handy actually, because there were enemy look-outs everywhere.

This was one of the other parachute skills that I was going to be teaching Colin and Harry – rolling over and over after you've bent your knees, so that you can quickly hide in the bushes.

Or snowdrifts. It depends on where you're landing.

I had chosen the snow of the

North Pole for us to roll over on because it was my duty as a leader to make Harry and Colin's first-ever jumps without parachutes as safe as I possibly could.

We would be flying to the North Pole in a plane that had been specially made for me. It was a plane that you could all jump out of together, because once we had jumped, it would switch to automatic pilot, park itself in the sky and wait for our command to swoop down and pick us up.

At 11.47 hundred hours precisely, we took off.

CHAPTER 11

**PIRATE POLAR BEAR
FACT FILE:**

Never play snowballs with pirate
polar bears. They are proper snow
villains that can't be trusted.

We were 30,000 feet up in the air
before I told them about the pirate
polar bears.

"First, we jump from our plane," I said. "Second, we bend our knees when we land.

"Third, we roll over and over.

"Fourth, we look out for pirate polar bears and, if the coast is clear, we do it all over again."

"What do pirate polar bears look like?" asked Harry.

"White with black eye patches," I told him.

"Are they dangerous?" asked Colin.

"It depends how many ice cubes they've managed to steal," I told them.

It was the very latest information I had received from World Defence Headquarters. Polar bears, worried about global warming, had been turning into pirates and stealing ice cubes from fridges all over the North Pole.

Eskimos had been taken hostage and only given back to their families in exchange for ice cubes.

Wildlife cameramen had had their cameras stolen and only given back in exchange for ice cubes.

If pirate polar bears managed to capture us and then take control of our plane, there was no telling how many ice cubes around the world would be stolen.

"Is everyone clear?" I said. "We jump, we bend our knees, we roll over, we hide, we look out. If the coast is clear, we get back to the plane and then practise again."

"And if the coast isn't clear?" said Harry.

"WE RUN!"

It was minus 100 degrees when we stepped out onto the wings of our aeroplane and looked down onto the snow.

"I can't see any pirate polar bears," said Colin.

"You won't unless they look up," I said. "If they look up we'll see their black noses and eye patches."

"GERONIMO!!" I shouted, leaping from the plane and falling through the sky.

"GERONIMO!! GERONIMO!!" shouted Colin and Harry, following my every move.

"BEND YOUR KNEES!" I shouted, landing expertly in the snow.

"KNEES BENDING!!" shouted Harry and Colin.

"ROLLING OVER!!" they shouted.

The drifts were deep, but our eyes could still see over the top.

"COAST CLEAR!" I shouted. "Mission leader to plane, mission leader to plane, we are ready to jump again."

Our plane picked us up in an instant, and in another two instants we were looking down from the wing again.

"GERONIMO! GERONIMO! GERONIMO!" we shouted, jumping off the wing on the count of three.

"KNEES BENDING!! KNEES BENDING!! KNEES BENDING!!" we shouted, landing in the snow together.

By our sixth jumps, we were all as expert as each other. By our tenth jumps, we were seriously thinking about forming a No Parachute Display Team.

But the pirate polar bears had other ideas.

CHAPTER 12

It was Colin who spotted the first pirate polar bear. It had managed to sneak up on us by covering its nose and its eye patch with both of its white paws.

How it got so close to us without us noticing, I don't know. If it hadn't suddenly needed to scratch its bottom, we would never have seen its eye patch at all.

The situation was much more dangerous than we'd first expected. A whole gang of pirate polar bears had crept up on us without us noticing – and they all had one thing on their mind.

"Tell them we don't have any ice cubes!" said Harry.

"I would if I could speak polar bear," I shouted, "but I can't!"

It was just our luck. I'd been learning to speak animal languages ever since I'd become a junior world defence agent. I could speak aardvark. I could speak badger. I knew how to speak camel, donkey, elephant, fox and giraffe. But unfortunately, I'd only got up to O in the alphabet.

"Try B for brown bear!" shouted Harry.

So I did, but it didn't work.

"Try K for koala!" shouted Colin.

So I did, but that didn't work either. The only thing that would work was proper polar bear language!!

"WE'RE GOING TO DIE!" cried Harry.

"WE'RE GOING TO BE EATEN!" cried Colin.

"MISSION CONTROL TO PLANE, MISSION CONTROL TO PLANE! COME IN, PLANE!!" I shouted, tapping frantically on the buttons of my radio-control gadget.

"OH NO!!!" I gasped, looking at Harry and Colin. "MY RADIO-COMMAND BUTTONS HAVE FROZEN!"

"WE'RE GOING TO BE MADE INTO ICE CREAM!" cried Colin.

It was as dangerous as dangerous could get. The pirate polar bears were desperate for ice cubes and had crept up so close, I could feel their hot breath on my cheeks! This gave me an idea . . .

THE POLAR BEAR'S HOT BREATH MELTED
THE BUTTONS BACK INTO ACTION!

"COME IN, PLANE! COME IN, PLANE!" I shouted, holding up the frozen radio-control gadget and using the heat from the polar bear's hot breath to melt my buttons back into action.

It was the stroke of survival genius that we needed. Thanks to my quick thinking, our radio control buttons were working again and our plane was on its way.

"RUN!" I shouted. "MY CONTROL BUTTONS ARE WORKING AGAIN! NOW RUN!!!"

All we had to do now was outrun the polar bears.

Luckily we'd trained for Sports Day at school in the summer so all of us were super-fit.

At 13.24 hundred hours precisely, our plane scooped us up from the snow, rescued us from the paws and claws of the pirate polar bears and flew us home from the North Pole.

We landed back at base at 13.26, cold, shivering, but glad to be alive.

CHAPTER 13

I like rain. I like the feel of it. I like the smell of it. But more than anything, I like the sound of it. Being back inside our den and listening to the sound of the rain is the best.

"Shoes and socks off," I said, waiting for Harry to crawl up through the tunnel before giving one of my most important orders of the day.

If you've been on a training mission to the North Pole, the very first thing you have to do when you get back is check for frostbite.

The way to check for frostbite is to take off your shoes and socks and pull each of your toes, one by one.

FROSTBITE FACT FILE: Frostbite is when your feet get so freezing cold from standing in deep snow, your toes start to turn funny colours and can even drop off.

If they are a normal colour, then that's a good sign. If they stay on when you pull them, then you know you haven't got frostbite and that your toes are going to stay on.

Thanks to our polar clothing, our toes, fingers, arms, legs and heads were all good to go.

Where to go next was the big question.

I fancied Dino Valley. Our training missions had gone really well that morning and I was totally up for some fossil hunting.

Harry and Colin fancied going to Hangman's Stream.

It's called Hangman's Stream because about three hundred years ago, a highwayman robber called Black Bill was captured and hanged there from a tree. The rope still hangs from a branch above the river, only today the body of Black Bill has been swapped for a car tyre.

Hangman's Stream is one of our favourite places to go in the summer, especially when the weather is really hot. If the big kids aren't around, you can have the rope and the tyre all to yourself, which means you can swing across the river all day. And you can fall in by accident or on purpose, depending on how hot you are feeling.

But today it was autumn. And it was still raining.

"It's not a very good day for Hangman's Stream," I said. "The banks will be really slippery and the river really wet."

"We're already wet," said Harry, standing up to show us the water that his bottom had soaked up from the puddle in the tunnel.

"There won't be any big kids there on a day like this," said Colin. "And if the river is up, we could do twig racing."

It was two against three. As leader, I could have pulled rank and ordered us to hunt for raptor claws in Dino Valley, but a good leader always listens to his men, especially men as loyal as Colin and Harry.

"Bagsy first go on the rope swing!" I said.

"BAGSY NEXT!" shouted Colin and Harry in a dead heat for second.

CHAPTER 14

By the time we'd cycled to Hangman's Stream, the rain was much heavier. The sky was getting darker and the light was fading fast. By the time we'd camouflaged our bikes with broken branches and loose leaves, the water was rising fast, too. Only the bravest of the brave would dare to swing across.

Luckily bravery is something I've never been short of.

I volunteered to go first.

CROSSING A RAGING RIVER

TIP: Before you swing across a raging river on a rope swing, check to make sure that enemies haven't cut the rope most of the way through with a knife. Then check inside the car tyre for booby traps.

The car tyre was wet and I knew that if I didn't get my feet in exactly the right place, I was bound to slip off as I jumped on.

The rope felt wet too, but with a

"Whoop!" and a "GERONIMO!" I went for it . . .

FEARLESSLY JACK SWUNG
ACROSS THE RAGING RIVER.

JUMPING TIP: If you are standing on a tyre, always jump off the rope backwards – otherwise it will get in your way and make you fall into the river.

The last time I had swung across a river this raging, I had been chasing a gang of illegal loggers across the Amazon. It was even harder swinging back after I'd captured them, with them tied-up and draped over my shoulders.

When I looked back across the raging river, I saw Harry and Colin waving and clapping me. I had swung about half a mile through the air, done three triple somersaults and landed on my feet.

"Now it's your turn!" I shouted.

"It's wider than an ocean!" shouted Harry.

"It's deeper than the Grand Canyon!" hollered Colin.

Colin and Harry were right. The water was rising faster than a bath with a hippo in it. But that wasn't all.

Think fins, think teeth, think danger!

"TIGER FISH!!" I shouted, warning
Harry and Colin immediately about
the bunch of killer fish I had just seen
swimming towards us.

"TIGER FISH HAVE GOT THE SHARPEST TEETH IN THE WORLD!" cried Colin. "WHAT ARE WE GOING TO DO?!"

"BOMB THEM!" I shouted. "SEARCH THE RIVERBANK FOR EXPLODING POTATOES AND PUT THEM IN A PILE OVER HERE!"

The three of us split up immediately and started searching the long grass and stinging nettles for highly-explosive potatoes.

"HERE'S ONE!" shouted Harry.

"HERE'S ONE!" shouted Colin.

In about five minutes, we had about ten potato bombs ready to go.

"PIRANHAS AND TIGER FISH!" shouted Harry, scrambling back up the slippery bank after nearly having his legs bitten off.

"HOW ARE WE GOING TO STOP PIRANHAS AS WELL?!" gasped Colin.

"FROM THE ROPE SWING!" I shouted. "LET'S BLOW THEM ALL UP FROM OUR ROPE SWING!"

It was a brilliant idea. Instead of just throwing potato bombs at the piranhas and tiger fish from the riverbank, we could score maximum bull's-eyes by swinging and dropping potato bombs onto their heads from above!

Harry went first . . .

I went second . . .

Colin went third.

"AAAAAAAARRRRRGGGHHHH!!!!" he shouted, losing his grip and falling into the raging river.

He had tried to drop a potato bomb with both hands.

"LOOK OUT! SHARKS!" shouted Harry, spotting a new and even bigger danger swimming up the river towards us.

"GREAT WHITES!"

he shouted.

"GREAT WHITES!"

The water level had risen so high that even bigger killer fish could now get into Hangman's Stream from the sea!

"I'M GOING IN!" I shouted. "WE'VE GOT A BUDDY OUT THERE WHO NEEDS SAVING!"

"I'LL THROW SOME MORE POTATOES!" shouted Harry. "THEY'LL KEEP THE SHARKS AND PIRANHAS AT BAY WHILE YOU GET COLIN BACK TO THE SHORE!"

I dived into the water, potato bombs exploding all around me. Bits of exploded shark floated past my face, making instant food for the piranhas.

SAVED IN THE NICK OF TIME!

Teeth gritted and lungs bursting, I struck out with some of my very best swimming strokes and managed to reach Colin in the nick of time.

"HOW MANY POTATO BOMBS HAVE WE GOT LEFT?!" I gasped, clambering up the bank with Colin on my back.

"THREE!" shouted Harry, racing towards us.

Three potato bombs was good news, but there was bad news to come.

"TIDAL WAVE!" shouted Harry, dropping the potato bombs at his feet and pointing up the river.

The sharks and piranhas were the least of our worries now.

"ACTION STATIONS!" I shouted. "Massive killer whales are coming to get us now! Look at the tidal wave they are causing!"

There was only one way to stop massive killer whales.

"We need to dam the river," I shouted. "And dam it BIG!"

There was no time to lose. We needed boulders, tree trunks, moss and mud. And FAST!

"I'll look for boulders!" shouted Harry.

"I'll look for tree trunks!" shouted Colin.

"BE QUICK!" I shouted. "And don't forget the moss and mud!"

CHAPTER 15

> **RIVER DAMMING TIP:**
> If you dam a river at its
> narrowest part, it will take
> far less time to do.

There was no moss in the fields next to the river, but there was plenty of ploughed-up mud. It was there for the taking so I took it in massive great clumps.

DAM CONSTRUCTION TIP:

Put boulders in a straight line right across the river – two lines if the water is really fast. Then put tree trunks on top, followed by more boulders to weigh them down. The higher and stronger you make your dam, the more protection from killer whales you will get.

"GOOD DAMMING!" I said to Colin and Harry as I dropped my first mud delivery off at the river. Harry and Colin had placed some humungous boulders and tree trunks across

the width of the river, and the water was already starting to slow.

"The slower we make the river, the slower the killer whales will be able to swim!!" I told them. "Start plugging the leaks!" I said, racing back up to the field to collect another hoodie-full of mud.

LEAK-PLUGGING TIP: Always pack your mud into the up-river side of your dam. If you pack it into the down-river side, the water pressure will keep forcing your mud and moss out. For extra hole-blockability, add leaves to your mud and moss.

After about an hour, we had blocked the whole river with a dam about twenty metres high. We'd used about two hundred tree trunks, a canyon's worth of boulders and enough mud to fill ten fields.

A whole pod of killer whales had arrived now, but even when they swam up to our dam wall and did a massive shoulder charge, there was no way they were busting through.

It was a complete victory, plus we'd done some of the best defence engineering the world has ever seen.

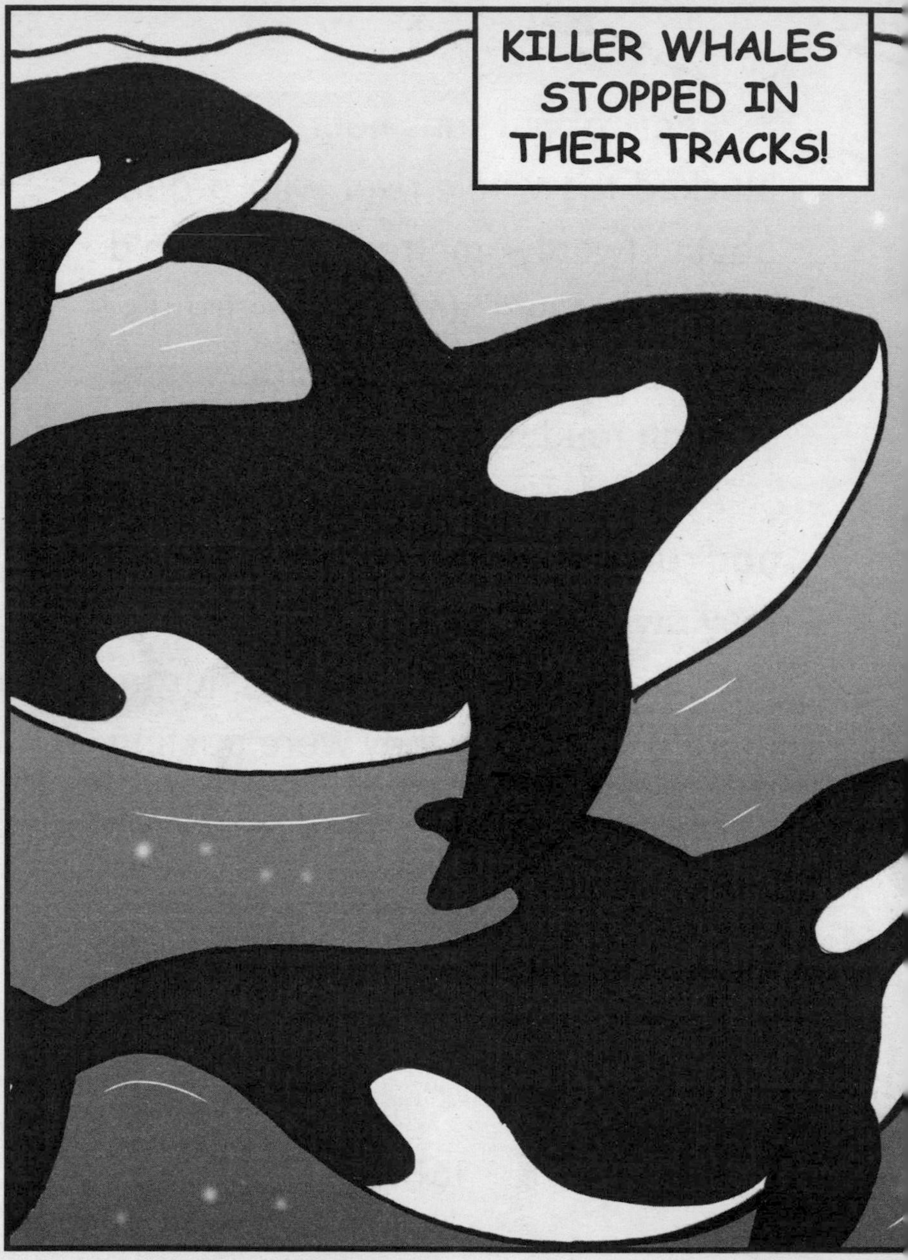
KILLER WHALES STOPPED IN THEIR TRACKS!

"I think I need to go home and get changed," said Harry. He was caked in mud and wet through.

"I think there'll be a killer mum waiting for me when I get home," said Colin, wringing river water from the sleeves of his hoodie.

We were all a bit on the muddy and wet side, but that's how training sessions can go. If you sign up to be a junior world defence agent, then don't expect to come home at the end of the day looking all neat and tidy. Expect mud, swamp slime, dragon blood, ghost guts, volcano lava, cactus juice, alien gloop and

loads of other stains that might never come out in the wash.

"I think before we ride home, we need to do a little more exploring," I said, clambering back up the bank and pointing into the farmer's field. "Get ready to see the biggest slugs you've totally ever seen."

CHAPTER 16

They were big all right. Fat, slimy, and juicy too. I'd spotted the first one over by a tree stump when I was looking for moss. I'd spotted three more in the long grass along the edges of the field when I was picking up big clods of mud.

"WOW!" said Colin. "THEY'RE MASSIVE!"

"I'D LIKE TO SEE A BLACKBIRD SWALLOW ONE OF THOSE!" said Harry.

He dropped down onto his knees and then pretended to do bird pecks with his fingers.

The slugs were totally humungous. They were about ten centimetres long and almost two centimetres thick across the middle.

"How big were the ones you saw in the Jungle of Lost Souls?" I asked Colin.

"NOT as big as those!" he said.

"Do you reckon they're poisonous?" asked Harry, giving up on his bird pecks, in case he got bitten.

"Yup," I said. "The orange line around their body is probably where they store their venom."

"HERE'S SOME MORE!" shouted Colin, stepping through the long grass at the edge of the field that  the tractor hadn't reached. "AND SOME MORE, AND SOME MORE, AND SOME MORE!"

It was true. The more the rain had fallen, the more the slugs had come slithering out. As we crossed the river to return to our bikes, a feeling of slimy danger began to creep over us.

"We need to get on our bikes," said Harry, "before they poison our tyres!"

"There's one on my saddle!" cried Colin, lifting the camouflage branches off our bikes and dragging his handlebars up from the ground.

"THERE'S ONE ON MY NECK!" screamed Harry, slapping the side of his face and then falling unconscious into the field. "Only kidding!" he laughed, climbing back to his feet and then staggering in zigzags over to his bike.

It had been a brilliant day, full of really good training lessons. We'd

battled combat snakes and hissing gorillas and pirate polar bears and tiger fish and piranhas and sharks and killer whales.

Who'd have guessed that our biggest battle was yet to come?

CHAPTER 17

Compared with Saturday, Sunday was a bit of a washout. It rained all day again, but what was worse, Harry and Colin had been grounded for getting their clothes wet and muddy the day before.

My mum and dad were too tired to do anything with me, after going on a really long mission the night before. I hadn't actually seen them since Friday, but when I peeped past the door into their bedroom, I could at least see that they'd made it back from their mission OK.

Not that I was worried about them or anything. They can look after themselves just as much as I can.

There were lumps in the milk and there was no bacon or fruit juice in the fridge on Sunday morning, so for breakfast I had nobby bread and butter. A lot of people don't like nobby bread, but I don't mind eating the end bits because it gives you more to chew.

My saddle was wet again when I

got on it, but after I'd cycled around in the rain for a few minutes, I just got used to being wet all over.

The rain fell in showers and spits. When it showered, I parked up under a tree or in a shop doorway, and when it was spitting, I just kept on cycling.

When I'm doing solo patrols, I try to keep as many places under surveillance as I can. Just in case something is going down that needs my attention.

It was all clear at the Bomb Hole. The Bomb Hole is the fishing pond at the park. Apparently the hole was made during the Second World War when a bomb exploded in the park.

I always press my ear to the grass

when I go to the Bomb Hole, just
in case another unexploded bomb
might have started ticking.

No ticks to report, though. A wet
ear, but no ticking.

It was all quiet at Hell Hill too. The lava that had melted my bike tyres the week before was so cold now that I could touch it with my fingers. There was no sign of the lava lions either.

There wasn't much sign of anyone anywhere. That's the thing about rain. It keeps everyone indoors, even the baddies.

When the sky exploded with a massive boom of thunder, I pedalled as fast as I could in the direction of the Dark Dark Woods.

Darker than the Blackberry Maze and lonelier than Dino Valley, the Dark Dark Woods are a place that only a fully-qualified junior world defence agent should enter alone, especially if you don't want to come face to face with a mad mad tramp.

I've never actually seen the mad mad tramp who lives in the Dark Dark Woods. Some say that his den is so deep in the forest that even squirrels are frightened to go there.

I'm not frightened to go anywhere, though.

"HELLO!" I shouted, trying to make my voice go as far into the trees as

I could. "ARE YOU THERE, MAD MAD TRAMP?!" I hollered. "IF YOU ARE, THEN SHOW ME YOUR FOREST SKILLS!"

Me, Colin and Harry had been trying to make friends with the mad mad tramp for ages. Every time we go to the Dark Dark Woods, we prop our bikes up against the same tree and shout the same thing into the forest to see if he is there. Don't worry, though – we always stay right by our bikes in case he tries to grab us.

As usual, I got no answer. Sometimes I even wonder if the mad mad tramp really exists.

When the rain got lighter and

the thunder stopped thundering, I decided to cycle to Scorched Urf. But when I got there, I spotted some big kids smoking cigarettes in the burned-out car.

Cigarettes aren't how the car got burned-out. It happened during an alien attack last summer. The car was scorched by the massive flame-gun on the alien mother ship. It fired at me when I was trying to drive Harry and Colin to safety. Luckily we managed to jump out before the whole car exploded into flames.

No one is really allowed to sit in the burned-out car apart from me, Harry and Colin. The thing is, though, if I'd ordered the big kids out and one of them had tried to get me in a hold, I'd have done so many really good combat moves on them I'd probably have blown my cover.

So I moved on.

And on.

And on.

Everywhere I went there were more puddles than people.

Devil's Weir was really foaming,

the long grass at the Blackberry Maze
was really squelchy,

and even the pit in Dino Valley looked
more slippery than I'd ever seen it
before.

It was a day for fish, not people. Fish and slugs.

The slugs were back again BIG TIME. As soon as I noticed one, I seemed to notice two. As soon as I noticed two, I seemed to notice four.

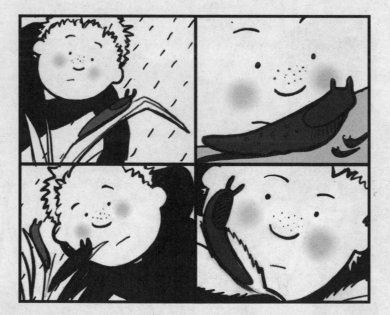

Some were big, some were small, some were grey, some were brown and some were black. All of them were on the move, though.

But where were they going?

And why were they going there?

It was 15.45 hundred hours. My knees were wet, my back was soaking, my trainers were drenched and my tummy was rumbling.

I decided I would do my next investigations from home.

CHAPTER 18

When I got back to my house, my mum was in the kitchen. She was too busy to really notice me, because she was cooking our Sunday dinner.

We always have chicken for Sunday dinner – chicken nuggets, Yorkshire puddings and crinkly chips.

Sundays are totally the best days to eat in my house, because once my mum gets back from doing the shopping, our fridge is full of really nice things to eat: frozen nuggets, frozen chips, frozen pizzas, frozen burgers, frozen pies, frozen fish fingers, frozen pretty much everything you can think of.

It's a shame they don't make frozen gravy, really.

After I'd taken off my wet trainers, I went into the lounge. My dad was lying on the sofa: his eyes were closed, his feet were stretched out and he was snoring quite loudly too.

It looked like his latest mission had really made him tired, so instead of waking him up to tell him about the slugs, I decided to go on the computer

and build a slug file of my own.

AGENT J SLUG FILE
Slugs: about 6 different types
Colour: about 4 different colours
Habitat: wet, dark or slimy places
Slime: loads
Bones: none
Ears: none
Feelers: two at the top for seeing, two lower down for sniffing
Extra invisible noses: 4
Favourite food: flowers, vegetables, worms, dead animals and even other slugs!!!!!!!
Teeth: up to 3000!

When I saw that slugs have up to 3000 teeth, I nearly fell off my chair.

198

I always thought slugs just sucked. I had no idea they actually munched their food with rows and rows of tiny invisible gnashers!

Everything was starting to make sense. If slugs had 3000 teeth, no wonder they ate meat. No wonder they liked munching on worms and other slugs and dead blackbirds. If I had 3000 teeth, I'd get bored of lettuce too!

When my mum shouted from the kitchen to tell us that dinner was ready, my dad stopped snoring and woke up.

"Did you know that slugs have

3000 teeth?" I said. "And four invisible noses! Me, Colin and Harry have seen hundreds of slugs this weekend. All different sizes and colours!"

I probably should have let my mum and dad eat their dinner before I started talking about slugs, but I'd seen so many over the past two days I couldn't wait.

"This is what you kill slugs with," said my dad, picking up the saltshaker. "You sprinkle them like this," he said, pouring a line of salt along his chip and then popping it into his mouth.

"Your dad's right," said my mum, doing the same with a chicken nugget. "Salt is how your granddad has always killed the slugs in his garden; has been ever since I was a little girl."

The telly was off and things were getting interesting!

"How does salt kill slugs?" I asked, eager to know more.

"It dissolves them," said my dad.

"Stops them dead in their tracks," said my mum.

"But how?" I asked.

"It just does," said my dad, picking up the TV remote and switching on the telly.

I didn't bother waiting to see what programme was going to come on. Whatever it was, it wouldn't be as interesting as slugs. And anyway, my mum and dad never talk to me when there's a programme on the telly.

I finished my dinner, went to my bedroom, sat on my bed and counted my teeth with my tongue.

I had twenty-two teeth, not including the gaps. Why then would a slug need 3000? And what was with the four invisible noses?

After going on my computer and listening to my mum and dad, I had got to know more about slugs than I had ever known before. But there were still loads of important questions that I needed to answer.

I thought about the slugs I had seen over the last two days. I thought about their colours. I thought about their shapes.

I thought about their SIZE.

I thought about their SIZE!

I thought about their SIZE!!!

Had the slugs I'd seen been getting BIGGER?!

If there's one thing being a junior world defence agent teaches you, it's not to panic. But the more I thought about the slugs we'd all seen on Saturday, the more I realized that something massive might be going down right in front of my nose.

The slugs we had seen under the rhubarb on Saturday morning had been small black ones.

 The slugs Colin had seen in the Jungle of Lost Souls had been bigger grey ones.

The slugs we had seen at Hangman's Stream in the afternoon had been massive brown ones.

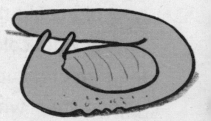

Could it really be that the slugs were getting bigger and bigger and bigger?

Could it even be that they were changing colour as they grew, from black to grey to brown?

And what if it didn't stop there?

If small black slugs were turning into big grey slugs, and big grey slugs were turning into massive brown slugs, how fast were they growing?

And if they kept on growing, just how big could they get??!!

And what colour next? Green slugs the size of a cucumber?

And then what? Yellow slugs the size of a canoe??

A slug the size of a canoe could really do some damage, especially with 3000 teeth.

And what about those four invisible noses? A slug the size of a canoe with four invisible noses could REALLY sniff for meat!

Not just worm meat, either. Or other slug meat. Or dead blackbird meat.

I am made of meat. If the slugs grew to a humungous size, they might come sniffing for ME! And Colin and Harry and my mum and dad and everyone else I know!!!!!!!!!!

Things were getting far more serious than I'd ever imagined. It was clear from my patrols on my bike that day that the fast-growing, colour-changing slugs from Allotment 24 were totally on the move. The question now was, where would they go next? And was there anyone in the world with the skills to stop them?

CHAPTER 19

When I got up for school on Monday, it was STILL raining! The weather had been on the slugs' side for three days in a row now, but it didn't matter.

I was totally prepared for anything. I don't mean that my school stuff was ready; I mean that my defence plan was totally buttoned down.

After my mum and dad had gone to bed, I had loaded a very special missile into my chimney. My missile-firing pen was ready for action too.

ANTI-SLUG MISSILE TIP: If the chimney on your house fires normal missiles, but you are not sure if normal missiles will work on slugs, unscrew the top of your missile, tip out the gunpowder and refill with salt.

I keep my missile-firing pen in my pencil case. It was given to me by Adult High Command after I'd singlehandedly stopped a meteor from landing on a load of nuns.

From the outside, my missile-firing pen looks just like a normal school pen, but when I click the top with my thumb . . . KERBOOM! The missile in my chimney is launched!

At 08.30 hundred hours precisely, I stepped out into the rain and met up with Colin and Harry. On our way to school, I told them everything I had seen on my Sunday patrols.

Harry and Colin were full of questions.

How big did I think a slug could grow? Had I actually seen one as big as a canoe? How sharp were those 3000 teeth? Could they eat through buildings? Could they sniff

through rain?

As a junior world defence agent, it was unusual for me not to have all the answers. But this was the total unknown.

To avoid a full-scale panic, we decided not to mention the slugs to any of the other children at school. Boys like David Alexander would probably not believe us. Girls like Daisy Butters and Gabriella Summers would probably wet their knickers.

The playground was full when we got there – full of children, full of parents, full of MEAT!

But when the bell rang, the children started waving and the parents turned for home.

It was 08.55 hundred hours.

The rain had stopped, but the playground was wet and slippery.

We were alone.

Alone in a school.

With only teachers to protect us.

CHAPTER 20

The teacher in my class is called Mrs Peters. Before I'd done a security check on her I thought she might have been an enemy agent, because she always keeps me so close. Plus she's always telling me off for looking out of the window during lessons. And for falling off my chair.

How a junior world defence agent is meant to see danger coming without looking out of his classroom window I don't know.

And how I am meant to perfect my canyon-crossing tightrope skills

without balancing on one leg of my chair I don't know either.

At first when I joined her class, I thought she was writing a close-up file about me to give to enemy command, but in the end I just realized that she was doing what loads of teachers do – trying to make me learn things I don't need to learn.

The problem with all the teachers I've had is, they don't know I'm a junior agent. They don't realize that there is nothing that a school can teach me.

But can I tell Mrs Peters I'm a junior world defence agent? Not without blowing my cover.

When we started lessons on Monday morning, no one in my class had any idea what danger they might be in, apart from Colin and Harry.

But Colin and Harry were still only in training. If anyone was going to save the school from a giant slug attack, it would have to be me.

Which is why I had to look out of the window instead of doing my maths test.

I figured it was going to be a waiting game. I had a good view of the playground from my desk. I could see the swings, I could see the quiet bench, but most importantly, I had a good view of the school gates too.

The one thing I couldn't see was the school nature garden. The school nature garden was ripe for an attack. It had been planted with lettuces and radishes in the summer and was probably the perfect place for a slug invasion to start.

Mrs Peters had started drawing sums on the whiteboard, but I was already doing some maths of my own.

How many slugs might attack?

How much time would I have to click my pen?

How many slugs could my salt missile take out all in one go?

If the attack started in the nature garden, then there would be no time to lose. I opened my pencil case, took out my missile-firing pen and placed it on my desk.

When I leaned forward and looked sideways as much as I could, I could at least get a glimpse of the gate to the nature garden. Or at least the red-brick pillar that the gate hinges were attached to.

As far as I could see, the gate was closed. That was good news at least.

I scanned the playground to the right: more good news. It was too wet to play outside. At least staying indoors would make us harder for a giant slug to sniff.

I turned to Harry and Colin. They were doing their sums.

I looked around the classroom. Everyone was doing their sums. Except Daisy Butters. She was copying her answers from Gabriella.

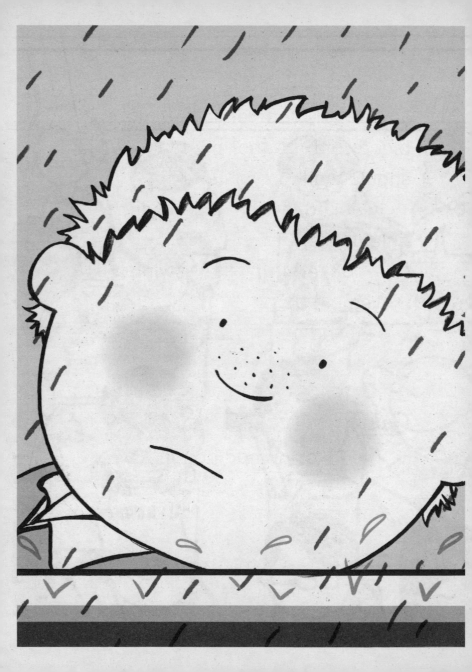

On the one hand everything looked so normal, and yet something in my blood told me that my long division should wait.

I looked at the quiet bench. All quiet there.

I looked at the swings. No movement there.

I looked at the school gates.

I looked at the school gates.

I looked at the SCHOOL GATES!

The invasion had begun!

CHAPTER 21

Giant yellow slugs the size of canoes were squeezing through the school gates.

"Under your desks, everybody!" I shouted. "The whole school is being invaded by giant slugs! Get under your desks and hide NOW!"

Mrs Peters was the first one under her desk. Harry and Colin stayed standing and waited for my first command.

"Sound the fire alarm!" I ordered. "We need to let the entire school know that we are under attack!"

Harry and Colin ran from the classroom to sound the alarm. I ran to the window to see how close the slugs were getting.

Eight giant slugs were oozing and squeezing their way through the school gates, and a load more were slithering over the playground wall.

"SAVE US, JACK! SAVE US!" squealed Mrs Peters, emptying her wastepaper basket and then putting it over her head for extra protection.

The instant the fire alarm started

ringing, the slugs stopped dead in their tracks. They obviously had invisible ears too.

"The headmaster is coming!" shouted Colin, racing back into the classroom.

"He wants to be one of your recruits too!" gasped Harry.

It was a kind offer, but Mr Copford would only get in our way.

"Tell him thanks, but no thanks," I said. "I've got all the men I need."

About twenty-six slugs were slithering across the playground now, feelers waving and gnashers gnashing.

"They look hungry," gulped Colin.

"They're sniffing for meat," I said, racing from window to window to make sure that each one was totally shut.

A giant slug was oozing over the quiet bench now, and the swings and the climbing frame were dripping with slug slime. Wherever they slithered they left a trail of sticky slime behind them. It was like the whole playground was being scribbled on by giant Pritt Sticks.

"They're getting closer!" shouted Harry.

"So is my revenge!" I smiled.

I removed my missile-firing pen from my pocket and pointed it in the direction of my house.

"TAKE THAT, YOU SLIMY SLUGS!" I shouted, clicking my pen top with my thumb.

The instant I clicked the top of my pen, a slug-seeking missile fired from the chimney of my house.

BLAM! it went, exploding in the playground and sending showers of salt in all directions.

The slugs were in giant trouble now.

"They're dissolving!" shouted Colin. "The giant slugs are melting before our eyes!"

It was true. Where once there were giant yellow slugs, now there were giant piles of gungy yellow goo.

"YOU'VE SAVED THE SCHOOL!" shouted Harry. "THREE CHEERS FOR JACK, EVERYONE. HE'S TOTALLY SAVED THE SCHOOL!"

All the children in my class crawled out from under their desks and started to cheer and clap me. Even Daisy Butters clapped me!

"GO, JACK! GO, JACK! GO, JACK!" they shouted.

"You're excused from homework for a whole year!" cheered Mrs Peters.

It was the kind of praise I had heard a million times before, but hey, it's always nice to be appreciated.

"Don't mention it," I said, putting my missile-firing pen back in my pocket and turning towards the window.

The giant yellow slugs had been totally defeated and would never come sniffing around our school again. The school caretaker was going to have a bit of a job clearing up the mess my missile had left, but at least the danger was over.

Or was it?

Or was it?

OR WAS IT!

I pressed my face to the classroom window and gulped a giant gulp.

"BACK UNDER YOUR DESKS! BACK UNDER YOUR DESKS, EVERYONE!" I shouted. "Another slug is coming our way, AND THIS ONE IS EVEN BIGGER!"

CHAPTER 22

It wasn't just bigger. It was HUMUNGOUS!

A slithery, slimy, sniffy and shiny slug about the size of my house was peeping and creeping over the playground wall . . .

But this one wasn't yellow. It was purple!

At first I could only see its feelers. But the more it slithered and slimed up the wall, the more its purple body oozed into view.

Its top feelers were as long as rounders posts! Its lower ones the length of rounders bats! All four were sniffing for meat.

"FIRE ANOTHER MISSILE!" shouted Colin, totally forgetting who was in command.

"I'm all out of missiles," I told him, pulling my pen out of my pocket and tossing it onto the floor.

The humungous purple slug was halfway over the playground wall now, and already stretched from the quiet bench to the hopscotch squares.

"How are we going to stop it?" gasped Colin.

We needed another plan, and we needed it FAST.

"Harry, Colin!" I shouted. "Run to the school canteen as fast as you can and bring me back as much salt as you can find!"

It was the best idea I could think of.

"OK, everyone, out from under your desks, including you, Mrs Peters!" I shouted. "I need you to empty your pencil cases and pull the refills out of all the pens you can find. We're going to make peashooters. Or rather, saltshooters!"

My plan was simple. If everyone in the class armed themselves with peashooters, we could load up with salt from the school canteen. Then, when the humungous purple slug came sliming right up close to our classroom windows, we could let him have it all in one go.

"NO SALT!" groaned Colin, racing back from the school canteen.

"The dinner ladies aren't allowed to cook with salt any more!" groaned Harry.

It was a disaster! Thanks to our school's new healthy living policy, there wasn't a grain of salt to be

found in our canteen!

"WAAAAAHHHHH!!!" screamed all the girls in the class, drowning out the noise of the fire bell as the tail of the humungous slug slithered and then slumped over the school wall. THE ENTIRE SLUG WAS IN THE PLAYGROUND NOW! It was about thirty metres long – who knows, maybe even longer, if you included the invisible noses. But the most scary thing about it was its teeth!

"Is the door to school reception locked and bolted?" I shouted.

"It is!" replied Colin, racing back from a security patrol.

"Are all the windows in the school shut tight?" I shouted.

"They are!" shouted Harry.

"Then cross your fingers and hope that it can't get in!!" I said.

All the children in my class were shaking like leaves. Mrs Peters was shaking so much that her glasses nearly fell off.

"IT'S COMING UNDER THE DOOR!" cried Colin, racing back from the reception area after doing a last-minute double-check.

He was right. The humungous, purple, meat-eating slug with four invisible noses and 3000 teeth was

squeezing its way through a gap no deeper than a CD case! I'd heard of giant octopuses being able to squeeze through holes the size of 50p pieces, but nothing could have prepared me for this!

"It's signing the visitors' book!" gasped Harry, racing back from the school office and looking as worried as I'd ever seen him.

I pressed my face to our classroom window. Sure enough, only the tail of the humungous slug was visible in the playground now. The front half had already slimed its way into our school.

THE FRONT HALF ENTERS THE SCHOOL!

"BURGERS!" I shouted. "Harry, Colin, I need you to run straight back to the canteen and fetch me as many burgers as you can find! No veggie burgers, though!" I ordered. "Veggie burgers aren't going to work."

I had a new plan, but if it didn't work, it would be curtains for us all.

Harry and Colin were lightning-fast and super-strong too, as they raced back from the canteen, each carrying boxes of beef burgers.

"OK," I said, ripping open the lids of the burger boxes. "It's time to leave a trail of our own!"

Harry was confused. Colin was

confused. Everyone was confused. But sometimes it's better for a leader to just lead and explain later.

"TO THE SPORTS HALL!" I shouted. "EVERYONE TO THE SPORTS HALL RIGHT NOW! INCLUDING YOU, MRS PETERS!"

We had no time to lose, and 144 beef burgers to drop.

"Everyone take a handful of burgers!" I shouted as the children in my class lined up and hurried out of the room. "As soon as you run past reception, I need you to drop a trail of burgers on the floor behind you, all the way to the sports hall!"

"But burgers are meat!" whispered Harry, holding out his box for people to help themselves. "If the giant slug gets into the school and smells the burgers, the trail of meat will lead it straight down the corridor to the sports hall!"

"Precisely!" I nodded.

"But the sports hall is where we'll all be hiding!" gasped Colin.

"Who said we'd be hiding?" I smiled.

CHAPTER 23

"FASTER!!" I shouted as my classmates filed out of the classroom. "GET TO THE SPORTS HALL AS FAST AS YOU CAN!"

"But we're not allowed to run in the corridor," said Daisy Butters, "are we, Mrs Peters?"

"Mrs Peters is already IN the sports hall!" I shouted. "Now do as I say, or else!"

If the people in my class needed

an excuse to run down the corridor, then they totally got it when they reached the school reception area.

"IT'S GIGANTIC!" screamed Nishta Baghwat.

"IT'S ENORMOUS!" squealed David Alexander.

"IT'S GINORMOUS!" shuddered Barry Morely.

The humungous purple slug was three-quarters of the way into the corridor now, and we had to run straight past it to get to the sports hall . . .

I raced into the sports hall at top speed, dropping burgers behind me as I ran. Inside, I found my classmates standing in a frightened huddle by the far wall. Mrs Peters was hiding under the crash mats in the sports cupboard.

TEACHER'S TERROR!

FRIGHTENED HUDDLE!

"We need to barricade the doors!" shouted Harry and Colin, putting their shoulders against a pommel horse and pushing with all their might.

"LEAVE THE DOORS WIDE OPEN!" I commanded, racing to the entrance of the sports hall and standing with my back to the corridor.

"THE DOORS OF THIS SPORTS HALL MUST STAY OPEN!"

If people were confused earlier, they were even more confused now.

"Open?" gasped Harry.

"Open?" gasped Colin.

"Yes, open!" I commanded.

"BUT IF WE LEAVE THE DOORS WIDE OPEN, THE SLUG WILL BE ABLE TO COME STRAIGHT IN AND GET US!"

"PRECISELY!" I said. "THAT'S PRECISELY WHAT I NEED THE SLUG TO DO!"

I ran to the door and looked back up the corridor. The slug had slithered out of the reception area now and was following the trail of burgers towards us. Its body was so big, it filled every square centimetre of the corridor. Its skin was so squelchy, you could hear its every slithery ripple.

"GET READY TO DO EXACTLY AS I SAY!" I shouted, glancing over my shoulder at the children cowering in the hall.

GET
READY!

There was no time to lose. The rubbery lips of the giant purple slug were just metres away from me now. It had hoovered up 138 burgers from the corridor carpet and only had six to go. Its evil eyes and slimy sniffers were right up close. I could even see bits of cabbage and lettuce stuck between its teeth.

"WAAAAAAAHHHH!!!!" everyone screamed as all four of the slug's feelers stared at them across the hall.

The time to fight back was NOW!

"EVERYONE GET DOWN ON YOUR HANDS AND KNEES!" I shouted.

"GET DOWN AND GIVE ME A HUNDRED PRESS-UPS!"

Everyone was frozen with fear. For a moment even Harry and Colin didn't move.

I had to lead by example.

I raced into the middle of the sports hall and dropped down on all fours. "ONE HUNDRED PRESS-UPS! JUST LIKE ME!" I shouted. "YOU MUST DO A HUNDRED PRESS-UPS NOW!"

"WAAAAHHHHH!"

screamed my classmates over by the wall as the entire slimy head of the giant purple slug squidged and squeezed into the hall.

It was closer than ever now, and it wasn't burgers that it was sniffing.

"DO AS JACK TELLS YOU, CHILDREN!" shouted Mrs Peters, jumping out of the sports cupboard and then rushing to do press-ups beside me. "IF ANYONE CAN SAVE US, IT'S JACK!"

Everyone ran to the middle of the sports hall and did precisely as they were told.

"DO A HUNDRED PRESS-UPS!" I shouted.

"DO A HUNDRED STAR JUMPS!" I shouted.

"DO A HUNDRED BURPEES!" I shouted.

"DO A HUNDRED SIT-UPS!" I shouted. "Crossed legs, straight backs, I'm talking proper commando sit-ups!"

"WAAAAAAAHHHHH!" screamed Sanjay Lapore as the humungous body of the purple slug made a detour through the basketball hoop.

"NOW GIVE ME A HUNDRED MORE PRESS-UPS!" I shouted. "WITH ONE ARM!"

"NOW TRY AND TOUCH THE CEILING WITH A HUNDRED MORE STAR JUMPS!" I shouted.

"NOW GIVE ME A HUNDRED MORE BURPEES!" I shouted.

"NOW A HUNDRED CRUNCHES!" I demanded.

It was the hardest exercise routine this universe has ever seen.

"My legs ache!" moaned Paula Potts.

"My arms ache!" groaned Barry Morely.

"NOW RUN ON THE SPOT!" I shouted.

"NOW SPRINT ON THE SPOT!" I ordered.

"NOW DO SUPER-FAST SPRINTING ON THE SPOT!" I commanded.

I was driving my classmates to the edge of exhaustion, but I knew that if I didn't, we would end up as burgers ourselves!

"WAAAAAHHHH!!!!" wailed Mrs Peters as one of the slug's giant slimy eyeballs pressed up to her cheek.

"EEEEEEEEKKKKK!" eeked Daisy Butters as one of the slug's invisible noses sniffed her cheesy socks.

"FASTER!" I shouted. "WE MUST EXERCISE FASTER!"

"But I'm puffed out," moaned Daniel Carrington.

"I'm puffed out too!" gasped Stephanie Brakespeare.

"Even my puff is puffed out," wheezed Mrs Peters.

"I DON'T CARE!" I shouted. "WE MUST ALL KEEP GOING! WE MUST KEEP ON EXERCISING FASTER THAN WE'VE EVER EXERCISED BEFORE!"

"WAAAAAAAAAAAAAAAAAAAAA-HHHHHHHHHHHHHHHHHHHHHH!!!!!" screamed everyone at once.

The giant slug was upon us!

"IT'S SLIMY!" squealed Gabriella.

"IT'S GUNGY!" squealed Daniel McNicholl.

"IT'S HUNGRY!" squealed Nishta Baghwat.

"IT'S DISSOLVING!" cheered Colin and Harry!

Colin and Harry were right. The giant slug was dissolving into a giant pile of gungy purple goo!

"But why?" gasped Colin.

"And how?" gasped Harry.

"SALT!" I smiled.

"But we DON'T HAVE ANY SALT!" said Mrs Peters.

"There's salt in our sweat!" I smiled.

All our exercising had made stacks of salt! More than enough to stop a slimy slugosaurus!

The school was saved. My job was done.

THREE CHEERS FOR JACK!

The caretaker worked all through the night to get the school de-slimed in time for lessons the next day, and when I walked in through the school gates with Colin and Harry on Tuesday, it was as though nothing had actually happened.

"TEN CHEERS FOR JACK BEECHWHISTLE!" shouted our headmaster in a special thanksgiving assembly.

"No cheers necessary." I waved, with a wink at Colin and Harry. "The only thing that matters is that you are safe."

SECURITY TIP: Make sure

that the entrance to your den is only big enough for you to squeeze through, otherwise enemies could crawl in and get you.

Allotment 24
our shed →

Way in
lift off lid
shelves →
water butt
old fork
window
Door
flower pots
jars
bottles

SURVIVAL TIP: If your den is

a shed on an allotment, cover your tunnel entrance with a hollowed-out water butt. This will make your entrance twice as secret and give you something with a lid to climb through as well.

CAMO TIP: When you get to your den, cover your bikes with broken branches to camouflage them while you are not using them. This will stop the enemy from finding and stealing them or spy planes spotting them from the air.

PRESSURE-POINT TIP:
Pressure points are special places on ambushers' bodies that make them fall asleep the instant you press them. But remember, pressure points aren't always in the same place. It depends on the type of ambusher ambushing you.

POISON FACT FILE:

Poison: One of the most poisonous things on Earth.

Combat snake poison: THE most poisonous poison in the entire universe.

EMERGENCY CUP TIP:

If you haven't got anything to pour your antidote into, make an emergency funnel out of a big leaf.

PIRATE POLAR BEAR FACT FILE:

Never play snowballs with pirate polar bears. They are proper snow villains that can't be trusted.

FROSTBITE FACT FILE:

Frostbite is when your feet get so freezing cold from standing in deep snow, your toes start to turn funny colours and can even drop off.

CROSSING A RAGING RIVER TIP:

Before you swing across a raging river on a rope swing, check to make sure that enemies haven't cut the rope most of the way through with a knife. Then check inside the car tyre for booby traps.

JUMPING TIP:

If you are standing on a tyre, always jump off the rope backwards – otherwise it will get in your way and make you fall into the river.

RIVER DAMMING TIP:

If you dam a river at its narrowest part, it will take far less time to do.

DAM CONSTRUCTION TIP:

Put boulders in a straight line right across the river - two lines if the water is really fast. Then put tree trunks on top, followed by more boulders to weigh them down. The higher and stronger you make your dam, the more protection from killer whales you will get.

LEAK-PLUGGING TIP:

Always pack your mud into the up-river side of your dam. If you pack it into the down-river side, the water pressure will keep forcing your mud and moss out. For extra hole-blockability, add leaves to your mud and moss.

ANTI-SLUG MISSILE TIP:

If the chimney on your house fires normal missiles, but you are not sure if normal missiles will work on slugs, unscrew the top of your missile, tip out the gunpowder and re-fill with salt.

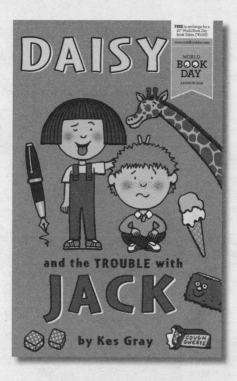

Daisy can't believe it! Mrs Peters is making her sit next to Jack Beechwhistle - the worst boy in the whole world!

Jack is so cross! Mrs Peters is making him sit next to Daisy Butters - she's such an annoying blabber!

As the school day goes on, Daisy and Jack think of more and more ways to get one up on each other. Trouble is, they might be more alike than they realized . . .

Specially written for World Book Day 2016!

The trouble with life is it's SOOOOOOOOO unfair.
Daisy's been grounded. No HOPPING or SKIPPING, FLYING
or PARACHUTING. She's lucky she's even been allowed
out of her bedroom after what she's done. But what
HAS she done that is SOOOOOOOOOO naughty?

You'll have to read the book to find out!

It's Daisy's birthday and she's going on a trip to the zoo
with her best friends, Gabby and Dylan! Best of all, Mum
has arranged for Daisy to go into the actual penguin cage
with the actual zoo keeper and FEED actual penguins!
REAL ACTUAL PENGUINS!

TROUBLE is, at the end of the day,
Daisy isn't quite ready to say goodbye . . .

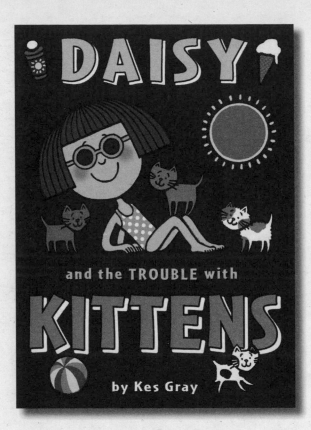

Daisy is going on holiday! In an actual plane to
actual Spain! She's never seen a palm tree before,
or eaten octopus, or played zombie mermaids,
or made so many new friends!

TROUBLE is, five of them are
small and cute and furry . . .